Dedicated to the King of Hearts -
you wily and generous trickster,
wherever and whoever you may be.
(And thank you for the flowers.)

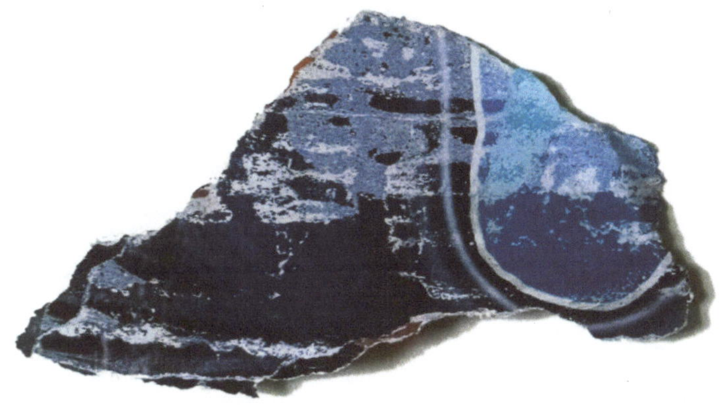

PAPER: A Tale of Berlin
Paula Billups

ISBN-13: 978-0692540565
ISBN-10: 0692540563

Bespoke Edition

Dragon Food Press
www.dragonfoodpress.com

PAPER

A Tale of Berlin

Paula Billups

FIELD NOTES DATE 20/4/16

I found this specimen in Berlin. I think it was near Kottbusser Tor but I can't really remember. I recently heard there are some microtemporal archaeologists nearby in Mitte so I visited their office, which was staffed by an old priest and a young priest. Just kidding. Except not really. The old priest was a woman, not really that old, but she sort of did look like a priest with wide black pants and a black shawl round her shoulders. Her assistant was a solidly built young man whose dark hair and dark clothes made his pale skin look even paler. She introduced herself as Dr. Gioia Arrigone and her assistant was Dr. Milos Minas, a postdoc.

When I showed the fragment, Dr. Minas lit up and exclaimed what a nice specimen it was. Dr. Arrigone took it carefully into her hands and pronounced it beautiful, but she was less excited when she asked to see my field notes and learnt I hadn't made any. These were bits I picked up over the last couple summers out of whimsy, thinking they might make interesting decorations for the offices – just never got round to framing them. She sighed and gave me these forms and told me to do the best I could, but that it was better to leave something blank than to guess if I didn't really know. So unfortunately for this set of artefacts I will have to leave some spaces blank.

I bought the blocks last month and have only just now had a

PHOTOGRAPH IN SITU? ___ YES X NO (IF NO TYPE NONE)

NONE

Site BERLIN MITTE

Artifact No. 001
ARR/MIN-BER0729-052014-BM001

Artifact Physical Description
Fragment of wall posters stuck together

Length 34 cm
Width 18 cm
Height 0 cm

Features

Fragment of aggregated wall scraps from advertising posters, type unknown. Noticeable features: bright yellow patch left side with "als" visible, white patch with teal writing and "nokratische . . .nda: doof." in black script. Right lobe is yellow with bold black writing, type unknown. Soiled and in fragile condition. Back of yellow (right) lobe says "Aufstehen statt aussitzen!" - maybe this helps with idenfitication?

Location Berlin. Exact location unknown.

Date Found May 2014

Weather unknown

Worker Brian Mistre

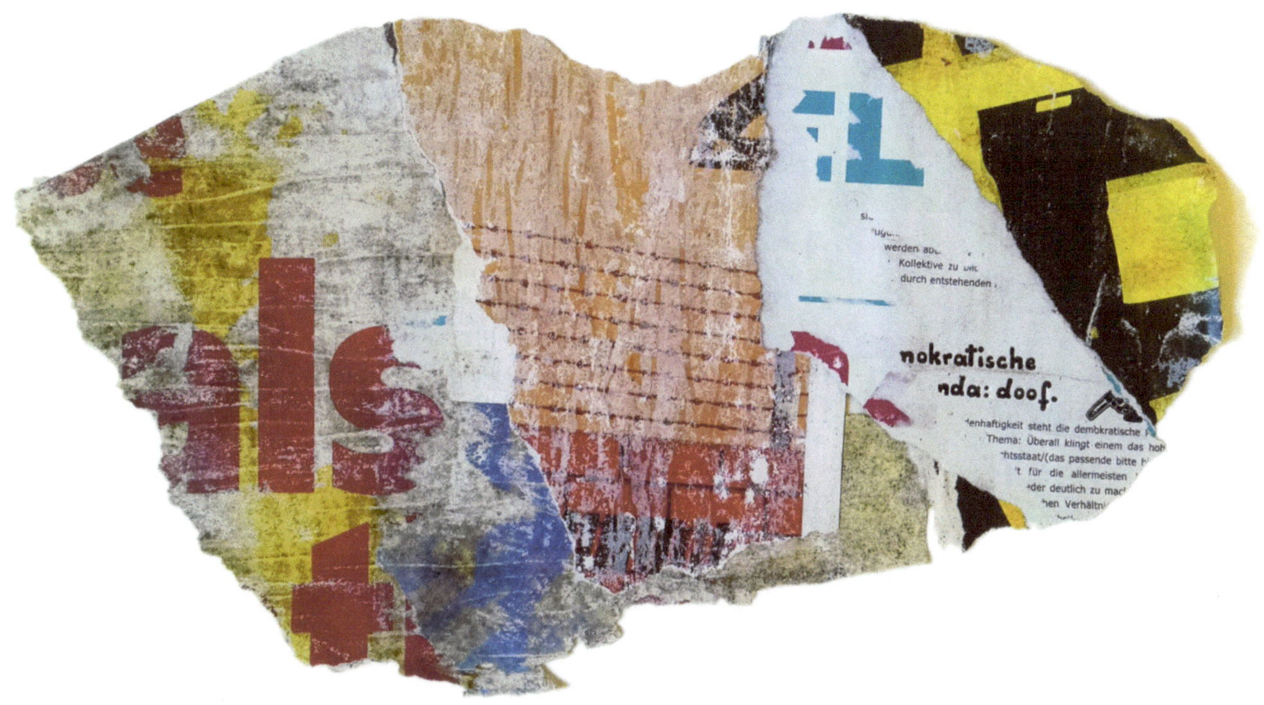

Field Notes, Cont'd

look round them. The wrecking crew want to know when they can start tearing things down. I know we need to get started on demolitions but there is a lot of intriguing material here. I probably would not have noticed only Lauren was reading a book about a new field called Microtemporal Archaeology, or urban archaeology of the very recent past. The book focussed in particular on a group of pioneers called NOW Archaology, founded by Dr. Arrigone. I remembered these scraps (they are doing nothing but gathering dust at any rate) and thought she would like to see them.

She told me to call her Dr. A., and Dr. Minas told me to call him Milos. He saw me out and reassured me when he saw I was disappointed that she hadn't liked the artefact more. He said it's a rather new field and most pullers don't even try to document the things they find, they just snag them. He said they were glad I came in.

We made an appointment for him to show me the ropes on documentation. They are scrambling to cover a site about three blocks from here before it gets torn down. I asked him if he had been to the Tacheles. He grinned and said yes, that it was pretty well picked over and that they were waiting for it to build up again. I realised too late that was probably a silly question.

FIELD NOTES DATE 28/4/16

Dr. A was not in the lab today but Milos looked over my paper and gave me a few corrections for notations from now on. The site has to be part of the artefact number, which seems to be a mashup of their last names, the city and the date of find, and the number needs my initials. Milos said they are mounting the 729th expedition in Berlin. There is a real motherlode of artefacts here.

Milos seemed startled by the personal nature of my descriptions of our meeting and said that Dr. A wouldn't like it. My feeling is, I am bringing them these artefacts, there aren't many notes about their finding, so if I note my experiences and impressions around them, isn't that something at least, and part of the most recent story of these things? I am mystified by all the taxonomy and numbering and precision that recording these artefacts involves. If I look at the bit of paper and see all the minutiae of its finding, it doesn't really tell me anything, does it?

I think academics just like having a form to fill in. But it only tells us, now, something about the thing here – it doesn't tell us anything about what it was like then. I will say I regret not having any in situ photos – that would give a sense of where the stuff was and why it was there.

PHOTOGRAPH IN SITU? ___ YES _X_ NO (IF NO TYPE NONE)

NONE

Site BERLIN MITTE

Artifact No. ARR/MIN-BER0729-052015-BM002

Artifact Physical Description
Fragment of wall posters glued together

Length 8.7 cm
Width 5.2 cm
Height 0 cm
Features

Very small fragment of what looks to be two posters stuck together, roughly triangular in shape, visible layer dark blue with a whorl of lighter blue on its right lobe, traces of paste clouding the surfaces, wrinkled.

Location Berlin. Exact location unknown.
Date Found May 2015
Weather unknown
Worker Brian Mistre

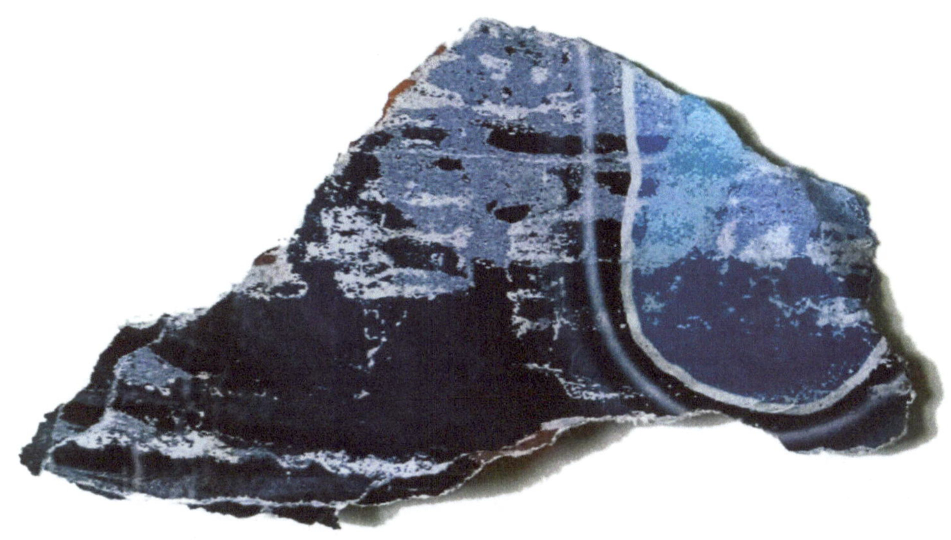

Field Notes Cont'd

Milos says he and Dr. A agree any information at all is better than none, and if I can certify it came from Berlin, and the general time I found it, that is something. He seems quite taken with the quality of the pieces.

Milos admits that I can write anything I want in the notes field – he says no-one reads them anyway.

I can well believe it. After he checked my notes and cleared this bit for being included in the research he wrote its number on the back, folded it in a piece of tissue and told me to follow him. We walked back to a storage room filled with white boxes in neat rows on wire racks, all carefully labelled. There was quite a large stack of boxes for artefacts like mine where the site notes are less precise. He put the wrapped artefact in one of the boxes, closed it, and we left. So much for the find of the century.

I've managed to put the wrecking company off a few weeks. They have more business than they can handle so they were affable about rescheduling. I'll make better notes from here on in. The dozen or so I have found so far will have to be incomplete images.

*Lauren is chuffed that I have managed to find a dig that is interested in the artefacts since I am only an amateur. With hundreds of expeditions in the city, I should think they would be excited that **they** found **me**!*

FIELD NOTES DATE 1/5/16

Dr. A was in the lab today and she looked over my notes. She laughed aloud at my mention of the young priest and the old priest. I am glad she took it in good part. I was feeling puckish when I wrote that - perhaps something of my Irish Catholic upbringing slipping through.

Less amusing to Dr. A was my attitude which she termed "casual" toward the artefacts. She pointed out that maybe we don't learn everything from these artefacts, but if we don't take care to classify and catalogue them correctly, then we could not hope to learn **anything** and might in fact draw bad conclusions. A good point, I suppose, but still, they seem sort of sterilised of their origins in the lab.

She showed me some of the more interesting fragments they had recently found and she asked me questions about the blocks I had bought and why I want to tear them down. I don't **want** to tear down the buildings necessarily, but some of them are so dilapidated they can't be left standing. Dr. A wanted to know where the blocks were and I showed her on the map - a few in Friedrichshain. "There are some really amazing caches of paper around there," she said. "Do you ever get down to Warschauer Straße?"

I shuddered. "I never go down there if I can help it."

Site BERLIN MITTE

Artifact No. ARR/MIN-BER0729-052014-BM003

Artifact Physical Description
Fragment of wall posters stuck together

Length 28.5 cm
Width 19 cm
Height 0 cm
Features

Fragment of aggregated wall scraps from advertising posters, 5 layers ~~thick~~ deep, type unknown. Noticeable features: pink and purple illustration of an old sailing ship on the lower right lobe, with the words "PANKE" and "TAKEO" visible (seems to be a fragment of "takeover." Upper left lobe deep turquoise with letters "IN" visible.

PHOTOGRAPH IN SITU? ___ YES X NO (IF NO TYPE NONE)

NONE

Location Berlin. Exact location unknown.

Date Found May 2014

Weather unknown

Worker Brian Mistre

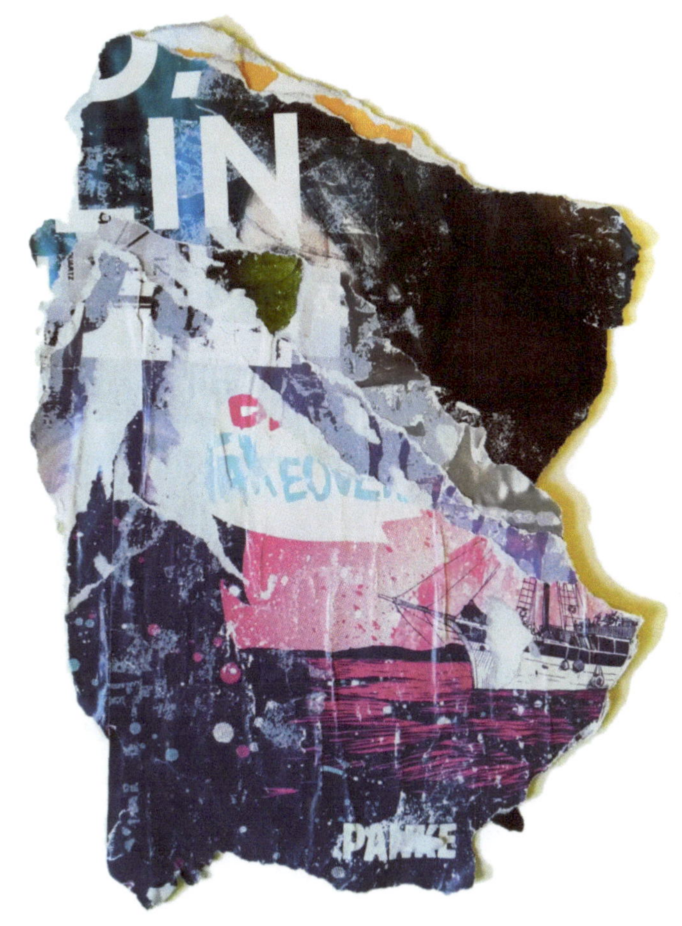

Field Notes, Cont'd

"How can you help it? If you use the SBahn or UBahn, at some point you are going to go through there."

I explained I have a driver. She grabbed a sticky note and drew the exact location of the cache she was talking about. "Difficult to get, but if you can, there are some really amazing finds there."

The only thing I remember about Warschauer Straße is that most of the people there are either half my age or twice my age, and all of them are drunk.

FIELD NOTES DATE 5/5/16

I am becoming a paper hound. I went out to the blocks yesterday to look round and saw that the workers had started fencing it off, preparing the site for when they come back in a few weeks. Without a hard hat I wasn't allowed in. I explained it was my property but the foreman didn't seem to care. I'm a successful developer and I am peering through the slats in the guarding fence like a kid who wants to get into a concert. I started home, and out the car window beautiful fields of paper were flying past too fast for me to see properly. I told the driver to stop and went home on foot. I bought a Bahn card and studied the station map to get back to Charlottenburg and my eye landed on Warschauer Straße, on the U1. I headed for that. A piece of luck - Dr. A's hand-drawn map was still in my coat pocket.

I forgot today is Herrentag. Oh God. It was absolute bedlam at Warschauer Straße. I came down the platform into the swirl of people twice as drunk as usual, old men in faded jackets shouting at each other, swarms of young women trotting past in moustaches and top hats, everyone in strange costumes. I pushed against the crowds and found the place Dr. A showed me. Light poles wrapped round with paper fifty or sixty layers deep. I looked at it helplessly. I need tools to get a proper section. The good news is they aren't going anywhere by the look of them.

PHOTOGRAPH IN SITU? ___ YES X NO (IF NO TYPE NONE)

NONE

Site BERLIN MITTE

Artifact No. ARR/MIN-BER0729-072015-BM004

Artifact Physical Description
Fragment of wall posters stuck together

Length 11 cm
Width 13 cm
Height 0 cm
Features

Fragment of aggregated wall scraps from advertising posters, type unknown. Noticeable features: glue-hardened and soiled, wrinkled. Fragment on lower left lobe is cobalt blue. ~~Fragmenton~~ Fragment on upper half is pale blue. Four layers of paper.

Location Berlin. Exact location unknown.

Date Found July 2015

Weather unknown

Worker Brian Mistre

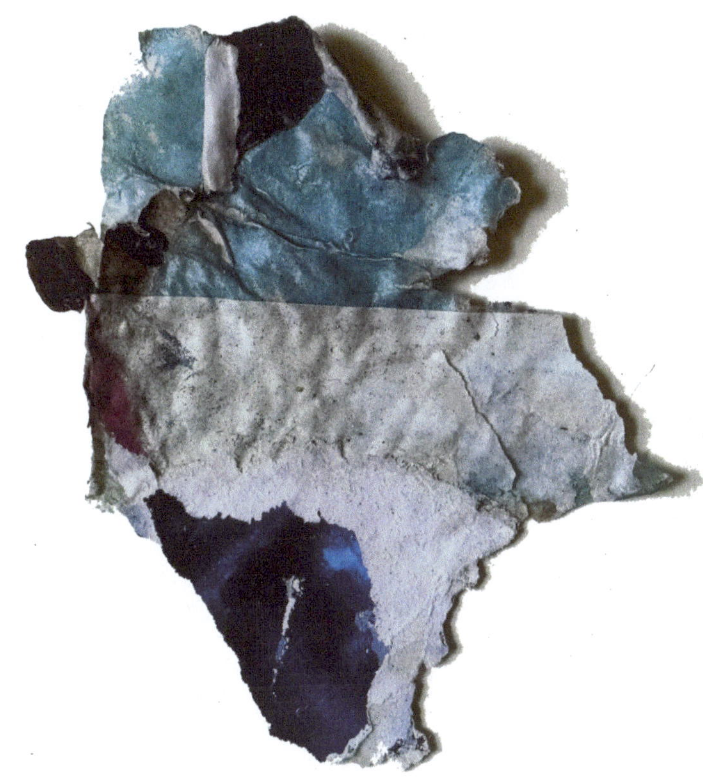

Field Notes, Cont'd

I passed a number of späties on my way, and feeling I should partake of the festivities, though I'm not a father, I bought a beer and drank it on the train going home. No fewer than three women offered me their company, and one man sat next to me and mumbled threats. I got up and moved off when he pulled a knife and started waving it at me. It was a tiny pocket blade, so his intention frightened me but his execution made me laugh. I could have thrown him off at the next stop before he used the thing. Still. Part of me can't believe I am going back there, but I can't resist, when I think of those papers like huge tree trunks wrapped round the light poles.

Lauren had gone out with her mates to be silly for Herrentag, but I hope she had better sense than I in choosing a place for revelry.

FIELD NOTES DATE 20/5/16

I keep getting distracted by paper. It amuses Lauren and mystifies my site surveyor, Evan. We were cracking along Rosenthaler Platz and he was trying to tell me what the builders want to do with a certain block, and I kept stopping and pulling paper off kiosks, taking pictures and making notes. Evan is a patient bloke, but at last he asked, "Brian, what are you up to?" I explained that I am gathering artefacts for NOWArch. He wrinkled his nose. "Who?" I explained that they are a new sector of the archaeological field that concerns itself with microtemporal sites. "What does that mean, microtemporal?" I explained that in a culture where the information flows lightning fast, microtemporal archaeologists see this as a collapsing of time. The amount of material a city block could generate in thirty years five hundred years ago can now be generated and presented to public view in a matter of hours, so Dr. A told me. We had been seeking paper out by Treptower Park and we passed one of the little cafés that hunker outside the SBahn. She gestured to the newsstand. "Think of it as slices." Dr. A is as easily distracted as I am. She grabbed a Mars bar and started to unwrap it, so absorbed in her point that she didn't notice me paying for the candy to the agitated stand owner. She pulled a knife out of her pocket, larger than the one the bloke

PHOTOGRAPH IN SITU? ___ YES X NO (IF NO TYPE NONE)

NONE

Site BERLIN MITTE

Artifact No.
ARR/MIN-BER0729-082015-BM005

Artifact Physical Description
Fragment of wall posters stuck together

Length 15.7cm
Width 21.5cm
Height 0 cm

Features

Fragment of aggregated wall scraps from advertising posters, type unknown. Noticeable features: At least 12 layers of paper. Lower half is a bright red field obscured with thin white paper, the letters (SS) and a fragment of another S. Small blue fragment in lower right lobe is blue and black stripes. Upper right lobe is evidently an image of tree bark. Lower left lobe edge bright turquioise.

Location Berlin. Exact location unknown.

Date Found August 2015

Weather clear

Worker Brian Mistre

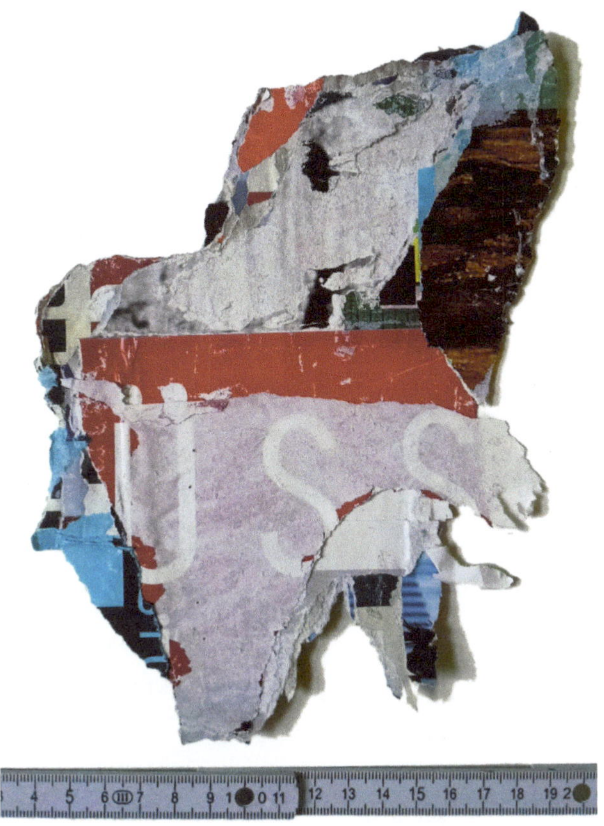

Field Notes Cont'd

on the train had waved at me, but the candy was the object of her violence. She cut a slice of it about the thickness of a matchbox. Then she turned to the stand manager. "Eine croissant, bitte?" He handed it to her and his eyes turned to me and I slid another euro across the counter at him while she cut a slice of croissant and showed me the two slices. "Think of it like this," she said. "If every molecule was an hour of time, this airy little thing would represent about a hundred years, and this dense little fellow would represent about a day and a half." I nodded. She offered me the two sweets. "Care for one of these?" I took the bread and she popped the candy slice into her mouth. "Mainstream media and other macro sources of information only crack the surface, as always. The real meat of what it means to be alive in this time is in the microinformation, the ephemera of private life. If a microtemporal archaeologist expects to record that side of history, they surely should do it now and not wait til tomorrow."

"But still, the amount of information is overwhelming, isn't it?"

"Yes," she growled in frustration and took another bite of her Mars bar.

FIELD NOTES DATE 22/5/16

I have taken a week off work so that I can get into the blocks and collect as much paper as I can. I told Dr. A I wanted to document today's finds and give them to her, but she said I should finish these entries first. She understands my frustration at not having all the field information, and seems worried that if I don't attend to these they may languish.

Still, I am anxious to take down all the treasure hanging off the walls of my recently acquired, soon-to-be-rubble blocks. I arranged clearance with the construction company to enter the premises of my own bloody buildings and have been tearing along. Since the workers have cleared off to another site I have the place to myself and it's both eerie and peaceful – just me and tonnes of paper. I now feel Dr. A's frustration. There is just too much of it.

I did, with trepdation and tools, head down to Warschauer Straße again, this time in the middle of the day, when there are fewer crowds and far less carousing. I took a saw and had at one of the massive accretions of paper round the light poles. I was afraid someone would stop me and demand an explanation, but I noticed people studiously turning a blind eye. Interesting. Cutting the section, it felt oddly as though I were doing violence to a living thing, like a tree, but I persevered and cut a chunk out and brought it to the lab.

PHOTOGRAPH IN SITU? ___ YES X NO (IF NO TYPE NONE)

NONE

Site BERLIN MITTE

Artifact No ARR/MIN-BER0729-082015-BM006

Artifact Physical Description
Fragment of wall posters stuck together

Length 14.8 cm
Width 6.6 cm
Height 0 cm
Features

Fragment of aggregated wall scraps from advertising posters, type unknown. Noticeable features:Middle of scrap has bright turquoise with pencil-thin black lines. Lower left lobe has a brilliant lemon yellow scrap. Fairly clean condition. 4 layers of paper. Upper point is a deep purple.

Location Berlin. Exact location unknown.

Date Found August 2015

Weather unknown

Worker Brian Mistre

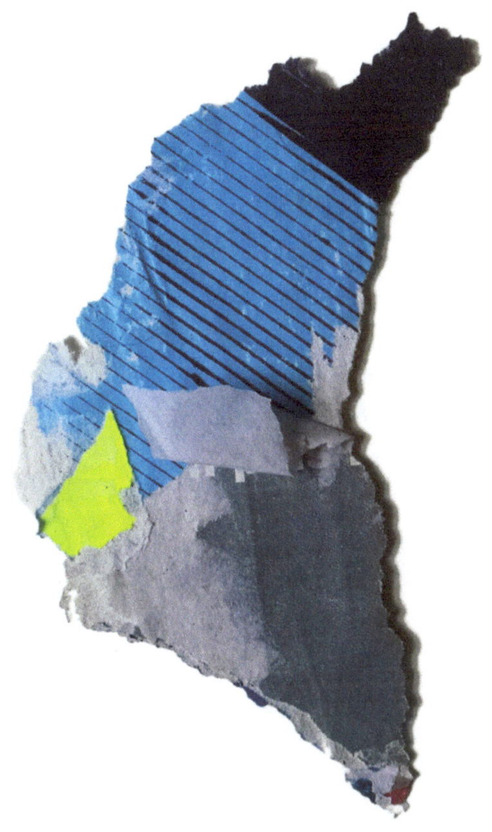

Field Notes, cont'd

Dr. A and Milos were both giddy and I was foolishly pleased with how proud they were of me for acquiring it. We divided the immense section into three parts and set to work documenting the bulks, then peeling them apart, layer by layer. I felt like a kid at Christmas and I think we all did – the oohs and ahhs as we uncovered fragment after fragment, silly, profound, scary, sexy, strange or just plain puzzling bits. I only got through a bit of mine because I wanted to get back to the blocks, and there was plenty left to sift through. Dr. A told me she would get a colleague to do it – I think she didn't mean Milos – and promised I would get credit for the find. I didn't care, it was so much fun working together to take them apart, seeing what was underneath. In all, it was over eighty layers! They barely glanced up as I took my leave, they were so absorbed in their treasure. I imagine they will be there all night.

FIELD NOTES DATE 28/5/16

I came in to the lab today with this report and Dr. A was irritated. "We are looking for layered fragments, not whole pieces of paper," she exclaimed. "The digital library has all the whole posters already on record. This will not tell us what we want to know, the cross sections, the combinations." She set it aside and excused herself. I sat for a while clicking a pen top and thinking about the last couple of days, how I gathered and gathered paper, knowing I could not gather it all, knowing that the demolition was coming, trying to save a scrap of today's history. My week off is gone. I saved what I could of my blocks, but I couldn't save it all. The graffiti alone . . . but that is another archaeologist's problem. Milos came in and looked at the artefact. I asked him if it was really useless. "Oh, no," Milos assured me. "We can get a lot from this sort of artefact. It's not what Dr. A usually likes to have in her archive, because it's not multilayered stuff. But you can get a lot more looking at an actual piece than if you were only looking at the library electronic file." He busied himself entering my data and preparing the paper. As we walked to storage suddenly it seemed pointless and stupid. "I don't understand why all the bother," I said. "Look where it ends up. Honestly, Milos, can you tell me that anyone will ever look at any of these scraps again, once you put them to bed in their little boxes and blankets?"

PHOTOGRAPH IN SITU? ___ YES _X_ NO (IF NO TYPE NONE)

NONE

Site BERLIN MITTE

Artifact No. ARR/MIN-BER0729-082015-BM007A
ARR/MIN-BER0729-082015-BM007B

Artifact Physical Description
Divided fragments of poster

Length 24 cm
Width 26.5cm
Height 0 cm

Smaller Fragment -
L13.4 W11.8 H0 cm

Features

Divided fragments of a single advertising poster, type entertainment. Noticeable features:appearance of gold picture frame on smaller fragment left and bottom edges, plus a red star. Larger fragment upper left lobe has turquoise back with large pink rose and red flower, marquee printing with the letters "2.5 S036 Entritt: 6 Euro - Beginn 23Uhr Oranientr. 190 Kreuzberg, Nahe U-Bahn Kottbusser Tor est zum Tag - der Paulheit

Location Berlin. Exact location unknown.

Date Found August 2015

Weather unknown

Worker Brian Mistre

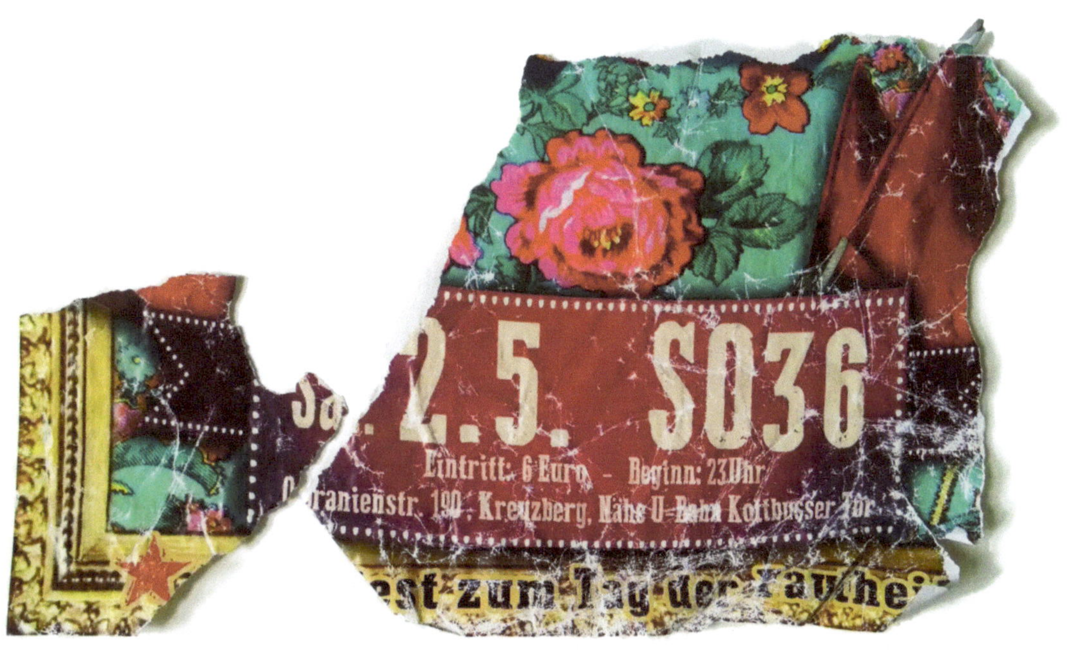

FIELD NOTES, CONT'D

Milos looked at me with large, calm eyes. "Probably not," he admitted, "but if anyone needs it, instead of being lost to the ashes, it's here." He gently put the paper to bed.

I apologized. "I am afraid I've disappointed Dr. Arrigone."

"Oh. No," Milos said. "No, she's sad. They hit the Tacheles with the wrecking ball today."

"Wow." I felt as though a wrecking ball had slammed into **me**. "Well. It's been closed for ages."

"Yes, but it was still a huge magnet for all sorts of amazing stuff. Artists from everywhere were leaving their mark on the building. Even if the Tacheles is no longer in operation, it was a treasure trove. Dr. A got wind of the wrecking last night. We were down there all night, saving what we could."

I gave a deep sigh. The Tacheles. I couldn't believe it. I didn't know what would cheer Dr. A, beause I don't know her very well, but I picked up a Mars bar on the way home tonight. I have stopped using the driver. I walk everywhere I can, and that way I find a lot more paper. Seeing it all slide by behind the glass of the car window was too much for me.

FIELD NOTES DATE 29/5/16 Site BERLIN MITTE

I felt sheepish bringing Dr. A another single-layer piece today, but I wanted to touch base. I have a temper and I don't react well to being snapped at, but I can excuse the grief that Dr. A must have been feeling. In the lab she was hunched over her papers in her black dress. She looked up as I extended the peace offering of the Mars bar and she silently presented a chocolate croissant to me. We smiled and traded apologies. "No, no, I was tired yesterday, and very sad, and you have been so generous with your time and help. Thank you so much. I'm sorry." I told her it was quite all right and she looked at this entry and recorded the data. "Looks rather sinsiter, doesn't he?" She was more relaxed than usual. "At a certain point the amount of paper is so impossibly enormous it will never get done, so you just do your little bit." She scrubbed her face with her hands. "I hardly slept last night," she said, "still burrowing through Tacheles junk."

I offered to take her and Milos to tea, and we went to cocoro. For once, all of us were either too tired, too sad, or too preoccupied to pull paper as we walked down Mehringdamm. At cocoro Dr. A looked round the tranquil cafe with its celadon walls and dark tables. "This is lovely."

I nodded. "You should never come in here if you are in a hurry." I ordered tea for us and invited them to stay and watch at the counter. Behind glass, the owner was making

PHOTOGRAPH IN SITU? ___ YES _X_ NO (IF NO TYPE NONE)

NONE

Artifact No. ARR/MIN-BER0729-082015-BM008

Artifact Physical Description
Fragment of wall posters stuck together

Length 30.4cm
Width 30 cm
Height 0 cm
Features

Fragment of aggregated wall scraps from advertising posters, type unknown. Noticeable features: large representation of a frowning male face, partial - eyes and top of nose - obscured left eye from overlying paper. Soiled surface. Black and white photo. Visible text says "Sie uns . . .Spende!"

Location Berlin. Exact location unknown.

Date Found August 2015

Weather unknown

Worker Brian Mistre

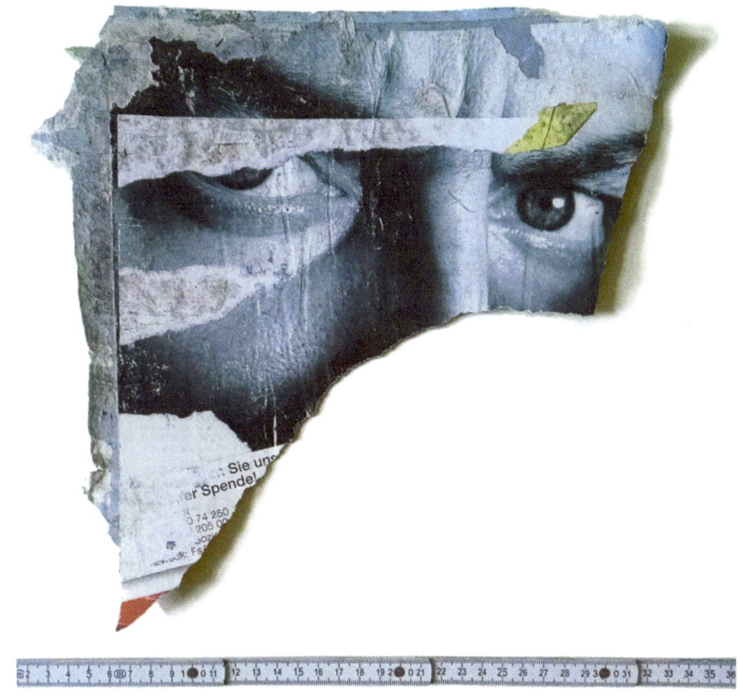

FIELD NOTES, CONT'D

matcha tea with deliberate care, in the timeless Japanese ritual. We sat in a quiet corner, away from the racket of Mehringdamm. I asked Dr. A how she came to microtemporal archaeology. She shrugged. "I used to be an artist. A painter. Then I came to Berlin for a residency and I stayed, and I started working with paper. It occurred to me this was a field of archaeology that wasn't being looked after. All data eventually degrades. So does paper, but in doing so it tells a physical story." She left art to get a Master's in Archaeology, and when it came time for her doctorate the field didn't exist. "I found a school in Switzerland that allowed me to design my own doctorate." That had been three years ago, and in keeping with the pace of the paper's movement, many others caught on fast. She smiled. "Plenty jumped off again when they found the job has no prestige, no funding, and no easy field work." But still the profession must have caught the science community's imagination, for it mushroomed, gaining legitimacy, the crowded field making scant funding even scarcer.

"You don't mind?"

She laughed. "Well . . . it's about the same as being an artist in that way."

I am glad that she laughed because it made us laugh, and we all need it.

FIELD NOTES DATE 8/6/16

Dr. A offered to show me some of her favourite places to get paper. We are all swamped, so we agreed to meet after hours. Lauren sounded intrigued, so I told Dr A, who told us to meet her at Yoga New Deli near Schliesesches Tor. Lauren raised her eyebrows. "**Schliesesches** Tor?" I nodded. She started to call the driver but I told her we were going on foot. It was like the days when we were poorer than broke and it made us feel happy. I like the return of walking to my days. We rode the U1 holding hands. We hopped off at Schliesesches Tor and Lauren looked around a bit nervously as we walked, but I pointed out all the places where paper was waiting for us - an MT goldmine.

At the Yoga New Deli, we sat on raw pine crate benches at rough tables. Lauren smiled. "This is fun," she said. "When is the last time we were in a place like this?" Before I could answer a man approached our table. He looked rather tough - long tresses flowing from a close-shaved mohawk, mysterious silver rings on every finger, dark jacket and sideburns shaved to sharp points on each cheek. Lauren had her eyes fixed on him. Although we were both looking at the same person, I had the sudden strange impression that we were meeting two entirely different people. I couldn't imagine who he was, but he addressed me in German-accented English and his voice was pleasantly resonant. "Hello, I'm Dr.

PHOTOGRAPH IN SITU? ___ YES X NO (IF NO TYPE NONE)

NONE

Site BERLIN MITTE

Artifact No ARR/MIN-BER0729-082015-BM009

Artifact Physical Description
Fragment of wall posters stuck together

Length 23 cm
Width 9.2 cm
Height 0 cm

Features

Fragment of aggregated wall scraps from advertising posters, type unknown. Noticeable features: mainly black and white and cherry red stripes. Shaped rather like a fish. No discernible text. Quite fragile. Four layers of paper.

Location Berlin. Exact location unknown.

Date Found August 2015

Weather clear

Worker Brian Mistre

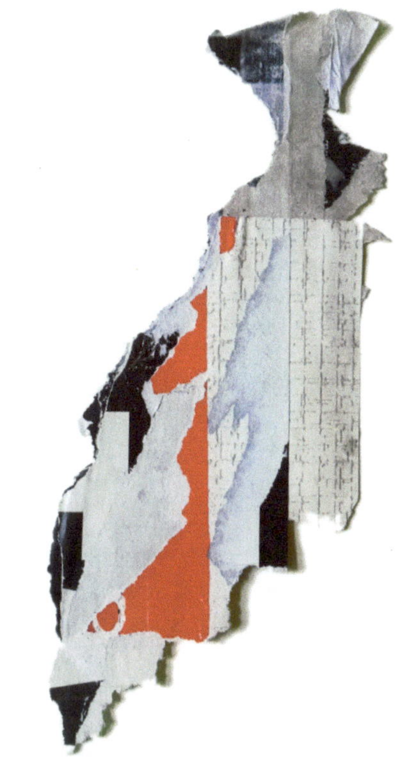

Alex Lorenz. Are you Brian Mistre?" I admitted I was. He gave a friendly smile. " I do research for NEWArch. Dr. A told me we would meet here."

"Yes, a pleasure, Dr. Lorenz, have a seat," I said. Dr. A hadn't mentioned him to me. The name rang a bell, but I couldn't place it. I know I would have remembered him. Lauren looked surprised and started to speak just as Dr. A and Milos arrived. "I see you've met Dr. Lorenz," Dr. A said, with a warm smile. "He was the one who finished your sample from Warschauer Straße."

"Oh, heavens, thank you!" I turned to him. "That was quite a job!"

He smiled and nodded at the thanks, and turned to Lauren. "I understand you're the one who got Brian interested by lending him my book." Ahh, so that's where I'd heard his name. Lauren gave me a mischievous giggle, and I grinned at Dr. Lorenz in thanks. Lauren is often ill at ease among strangers, but Alex had tactfully and instantly made her part of our group. We got better acquainted over bowls of macrobiotic food and then went out into the Berlin night.

At Kottbusser Tor, Dr. A handed black duffels to me and Lauren. "Milos and Alex will pair up with you and do documentation," she said, "And I'll do elevations and tracking." She orbited us as Milos photographed and documented my pulls and Alex helped Lauren.

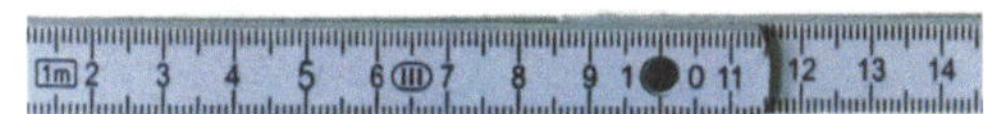

"I never got to ask you how you got to be a microtemporal archaeologist," I told Milos.

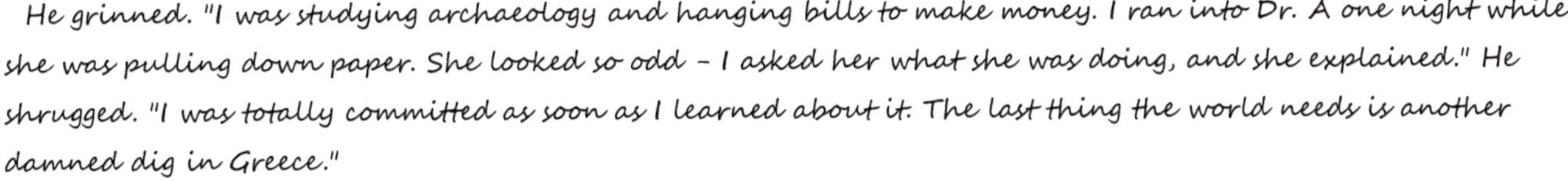

He grinned. "I was studying archaeology and hanging bills to make money. I ran into Dr. A one night while she was pulling down paper. She looked so odd – I asked her what she was doing, and she explained." He shrugged. "I was totally committed as soon as I learned about it. The last thing the world needs is another damned dig in Greece."

"I assumed you were Greek, with a name like Minas."

"I am. But I grew up in Paris and I was educated at Uni Potsdam." He chinned air at me in a warning and handed a pair of latex gloves to me from his pocket.

"Never pull paper below the waist without these, mate."

FIELD NOTES DATE 18/6/16

I am terribly excited because for the first time I can turn in a completed field form (all except for the in situ photo.) I have a record of finding this fragment in my journal, so I know the date and even the location and the weather. It's not Dr. A's usual fare, but I am hoping she will find this interesting. It was a memorable evening because I saw the man, if at a distance. He was hard to miss. Rather old, dressed like a king, stumping along on his walking staff. He did a street performance for a young couple and then handed them a paper. As I walked toward them, the girl said something angry, and the boy laughed. She tore the paper to pieces and left. He stopped to pick up the bits but when she stormed off he went after her. This bit flew to the ground. The errant king strode on his way. I wondered what the MTs would make of his paper.

(Appended) -- I showed the page to Dr. A and Milos and Alex, and I did not expect their reaction. Alex grinned broadly, Milos cursed softly in French, and Dr. A turned very pale. "Where did you find this?" she demanded. I indicated the sheet. "there, as I said, Senefelder Platz."

"Oh my god," she said, and dropped into a chair. "Again."

"What?"

PHOTOGRAPH IN SITU? ___ YES _X_ NO (IF NO TYPE NONE)

NONE

Site BERLIN MITTE

Artifact No. ARR/MIN-BER0729-23052015-BM010

Artifact Physical Description paper fragment, two-sided printing

Length 7.6cm

Width 7.6 cm

Height 0 cm

Features

Fragment of promotional flyer from street performer. Noticeable features: looks like fake Euro currency, with images of a white-haired, ~~beareded~~ bearded man wearing a crown and holding a scepter on one side and a half-image of what seems to be the same man ~~laughign~~ laughing or sticking out his tongue. Browns and yellows and reds.

Location Berlin. Prenzlauerberg near Senefelder Platz.

Date Found May 23, 2015

Weather clear

Worker Brian Mistre

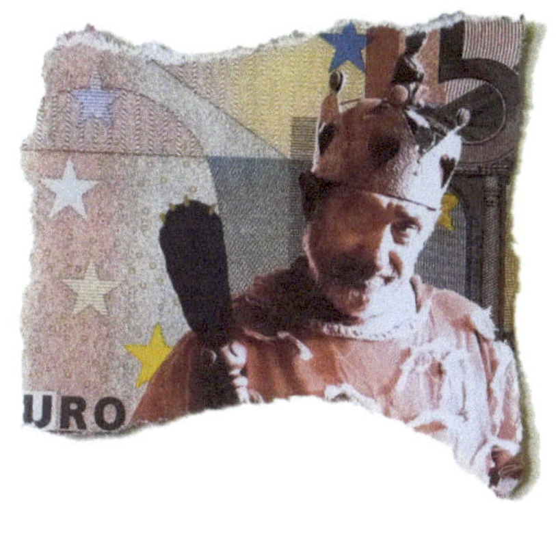

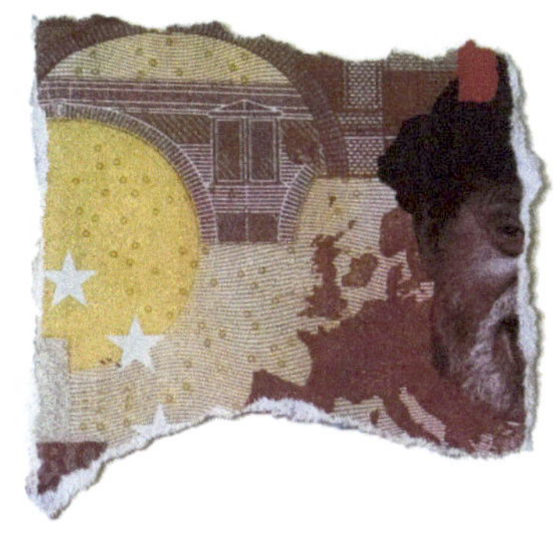

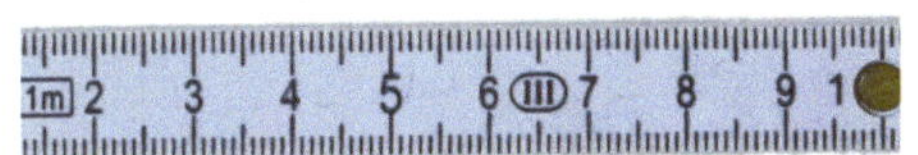

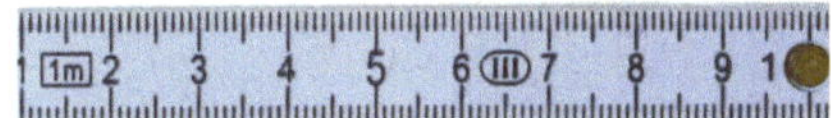

Field Notes, Cont'd

She shook her head. "This guy. This GUY. He's my white whale, my bigfoot, my Loch Ness monster rolled into one. He's some kind of myth. He gets spotted by amateurs sometimes but he must have the worst advertising strategy in the world." She got up and went to the lab fridge and unselfconsciously produced a bottle of tequila, poured four shots, and offered to us. We sat around the paper-drifted lab table, toasted and drank. Wordlessly, Dr. A poured us another. It was after hours, what the hell. I drank it off.

Alex toasted with us but set his shot aside untouched. "Archaeologists are not so superstitious," he said. "But he's different. We find his traces everywhere, but not one of us has ever seen him."

Dr. A sighed in agreement. "Seven hundred and eighty three groups in the city. Not a goddamn one of us can get a whiff of him." She shook her head vigorously. "It's completely inexplicable. It's like he's invisible to microtemporals. and you saw him. You actually SAW him."

Milos gazed morosely into his empty shot glass. "He's the talk of all the MTs. If a fragment of his turns up, you're supposed to have a good stiff drink. Or three."

I nodded. The excellent tequila lent sense to this weird tale. "Okay. Is that supposed to flush him out?"

Milos shrugged. "It hasn't yet," he said. "But it makes us feel better about missing him by a whisker. Again."

"Who IS he?"

Dr A. fixed a bright stare on me. "He's a performance artist of some kind. We call him the King of Hearts."

Milos reached for the bottle and poured again. We clinked glasses gravely.

Only Alex smiled. "Come out, come out, wherever you are."

FIELD NOTES DATE 25/6/16

The appearance of the King of Hearts set off a tremor in the community. My little scrap of contribution started the speculation afresh. But it seemed to me that there was not much to go on and a lot of MTs did their share of drinking that week. One reason his fragments cause so much fuss is the KoH does his own printing, so nothing of his is in the database. The weird part was that not only has no microtemporal personally caught fragments of his, they have never even seen him. Alex connected me with MTs, even though I had already written what happened to me in the report. Lauren told me that he had appeared to her one time, but she hadn't thought it worth mentioning. If one stopped to remark on all the strange and gifted creatures one meets in Berlin, one would not have time to sleep or eat.

Lauren and I had a holiday in the medieval town of Quedlinburg. In such an old place the paper was conspicuious in its absence. In a Greek restaurant, housed in fachwerk timber, we talked of paper. "I've been reading about the MTs," she said. "There are lots of divisions. Some track traces of defunct websites. Some are black hats that find when news sites have been altered. Lots of electronic data – almost none of it on paper. Dr. A and Milos and Alex have integrity. It's hard to get funding if you aren't mining data."

PHOTOGRAPH IN SITU? ___ YES _X_ NO (IF NO TYPE NONE)

NONE

Site BERLIN MITTE

Artifact No. ARR/MIN-BER0729-052015-BM011

Artifact Physical Description
Fragment of wall posters stuck together

Length 34.5cm

Width 15.5cm

Height 0 cm

Features
Fragment of aggregated wall scraps from advertising posters, type unknown. Lozenge shape. Noticeable features:two diagonal stripes of white - paper overlay - irregular edges - right half is a partial iimage of a man with his hand on his throat. Text in lower lobe: "lassen." Scrap of text in upper left region, few whole words, white on black text. uzbe.reife.. die ..Uhr aus..ler Mariann ..enkel beschreie...ahrige Poli..st an gleic...urde sie...Fur...sagt ier neru be

Location Berlin. Exact location unknown.

Date Found May 2015

Weather unknown

Worker Brian Mistre

Field Notes, cont'd

"But they **are** mining data – perhaps more personal and poignant than what one orders on Amazon."

Lauren shrugged. "Is it more poignant to have a record of the concerts a city mounted and the expositions they sponsored?"

"It isn't just that. Cross-referencing the demographic data gives a rich mosaic of a brief time. Things change so fast in Berlin. Microcultures blip in and out."

Lauren nodded. "Alex says that Berlin in particular is sort of intuitively spectacular at creating those kinds of matrices."

"Dr. A says that it probably has to do something with the stifling social conditions of the Third Reich and the DDR. People were totally controlled for fifty years. Now they have a voice, they are using it. Not just over dinner tables or in lecture halls. They are shouting what is important to them, from the streets themselves."

"Not to mention graffiti," she said. "The ones who specialize in that are as busy as the paper MTs like Dr. A. It vanishes lightning fast."

"Sometimes they say we are at the end of history," I said, as our moussaka arrived. "I think it's only the field of existence has shifted position and the way historians consider it hasn't caught up."

Lauren squinted into the candlelight. "There are international conferences where these guys compare notes. I'd love to be a fly on the wall for that. What's the paper like in Albania?"

That put an idea into my head, but it could wait til we got back to Berlin.

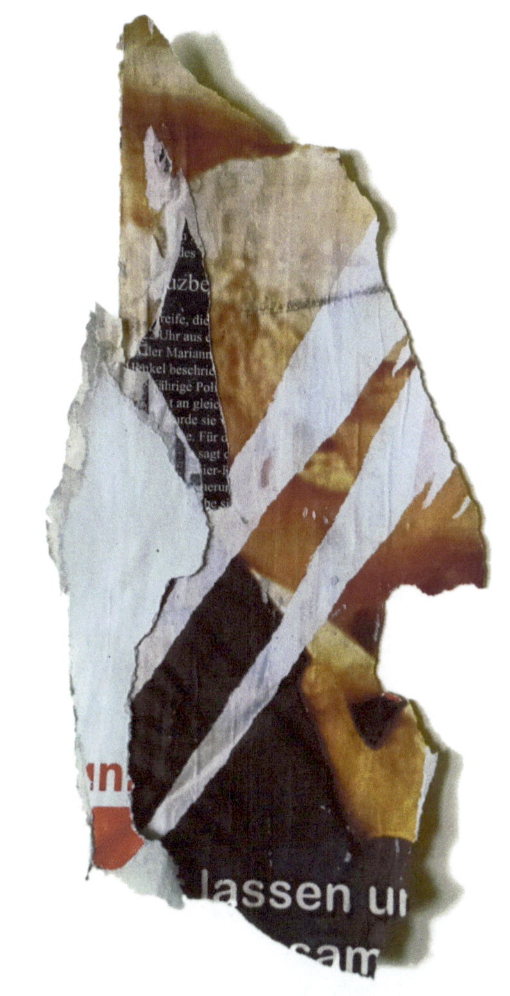

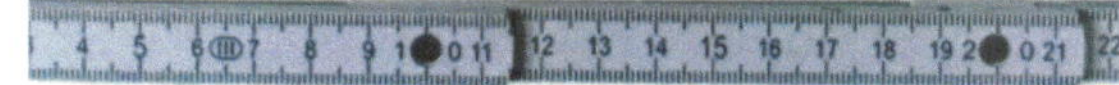

FIELD NOTES | DATE 20/7/16 | Site BERLIN MITTE

I was gone from the lab several weeks as demolitions got under way. My office is in a trailer near the site and I could hear the incessant crashing. I sometimes went to see the buildings fall. In five old city blocks, some of their buildings had to come down, and the rest were under massive renovation and restoration. Lauren worried and set traps to lure out any lurking cats. I told her she was likely only attracting possums and rats. "They have families," she said defensively. I love her.

I returned to the lab yesterday to drop off this fragment and Dr. A was not there. Milos looked more frazzled than I had ever seen him.

"Dr A is ill," he said, "I've been here a lot more." I don't think he was complaining. Over the last few months it's clear how devoted they are to each other.

"What is the matter?"

"She has Churg-Strauss Syndrome." Milos took a sip of coffee. "It's a rare form of vasculitis. The blood vessels constrict, limiting oxygen in the body. It becomes hard to breathe."

I was appalled, thinking of my body choking off its own oxygen. I felt a lump crawl into my throat. "Oh my god."

Milos nodded and took my fragment and entered the data while I stood by, not knowing what to say.

PHOTOGRAPH IN SITU? ___ YES _X_ NO (IF NO TYPE NONE)

NONE

Artifact No ARR/MIN-BER0729-082015-BM012

Artifact Physical Description
Fragment of wall posters stuck together

Length 26 cm
Width 22 cm
Height 0 cm

Features

Fragment of aggregated wall scraps from advertising posters, type: entertainment. Noticeable features: red, white and black colors predominant. At least four layers. Upper lobe a red field with the partial "neukoll" and partial text down the centre - "ng..lec..hangou..ie scre" Lower left lobe ~~hs~~ has partial text: "Kritisc..forum..Mieten Stopr . ." Probably found in Neukolln.

Location Berlin. Exact location unknown.

Date Found August 2015

Weather unknown

Worker Brian Mistre

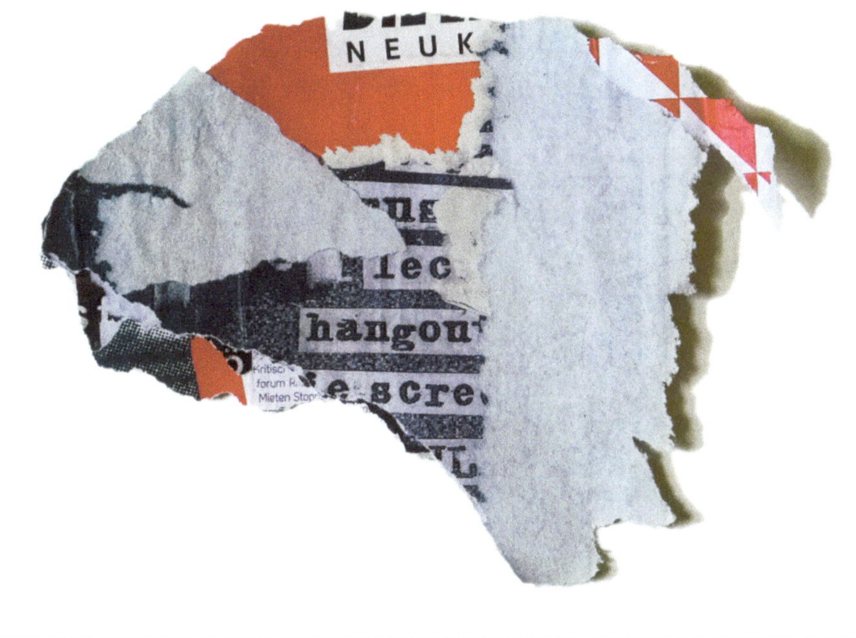

Field Notes, Cont'd

"Where is she?"

"In the hospital in Schoneberg. I'll go there in a little while if you want to come with me." We bought flowers for her, and on an impulse at the flower shop I got a stuffed dog for her. I must have looked defensive about buying a silly plush toy, because Milos smiled reassuringly said, "Yeah, I love her too." It's true. Dr. A can be gruff, but she is very lovable. We got to her hospital room and she was sound asleep and breathing oxygen. She looked paler and younger in the white and blue gown, without her makeup. Milos patted me on the back.

"Don't worry. It isn't the first time. She will be all right, she just needs rest. Working too damned hard."

We sat out in a waiting room drinking cups of coffee. I asked, "Does she have any family?"

"I don't think so. I've never heard her mention any parents or siblings. She's not married." Milos looked down at his hands in his lap and we couldn't think of much else to say, but I thought to myself, she has you, mate. And me and Alex. About an hour later we looked in on her. She was still asleep. But Milos said she would be glad we'd come. "She'll be fairly weak for a little while, maybe a few weeks," he said. "But she'll get back from it. They have a medicine that controls it."

"**Controls** it??"

"Well, sometimes. It's not an easy medicine to take."

FIELD NOTES DATE 29/7/16 Site BERLIN MITTE

Dr. A was in hospital for a week. Milos told me she was at work next day, but after an hour had gone home again. I called at her house in Schoneberg, and I brought this fragment along. She was tired and pale but her computer was on and she was working. She was glad to see me and even more glad, I think, to see the paper in my hands. She called it lovely and did the entry right then. I don't see any more what makes this fragment any lovelier than any of the thousands or millions to be got in the city, but I admit seeing her ill made it hard for me to feel excited about field work. "Dr. A, what happens in the end, when these fragments finally make a story?"

She looked at me. "They already make a story."

"Well - not really - there are no revelations. No . . . arc."

"Oh, Brian," she smiled, "there are no arcs. When did my arc begin? When I was born? When I became an artist? Does it start now, when I make you a cup of tea? Narratives are for stories, not real life. The paper tells a story, and the metadata tells us more. But there will never be an 'ah-ha! So that's what it was all about.' You can forget that in your calculations."

"Then why collect and curate this endless sea of paper?"

She laughed."'I can't explain it any more than you can explain why you bring me these fragments or why the King of Hearts walks around the city."

PHOTOGRAPH IN SITU? ___ YES X NO (IF NO TYPE NONE)

NONE

Artifact No.
ARR/MIN-BER0729-072015-BM013

Artifact Physical Description
Fragment of wall posters stuck together

Length 27.8cm
Width 43 cm
Height 0 cm
Features

Fragment of aggregated wall scraps from advertising posters, type entertainment. Seven layers. Noticeable features: Predominately black and white with bright yellow. Upper right lobe is a bright yellow triangle. Not much readable text, ~~exect~~ except for a"CLUB" in ~~teh~~ the lower center lobe. Left lobe text "& SE REI - COL" Some clouding from pastre residue on centre-right lower lobe.

Location
Berlin. Exact location unknown.

Date Found
July 2015

Weather
unknown

Worker
Brian Mistre

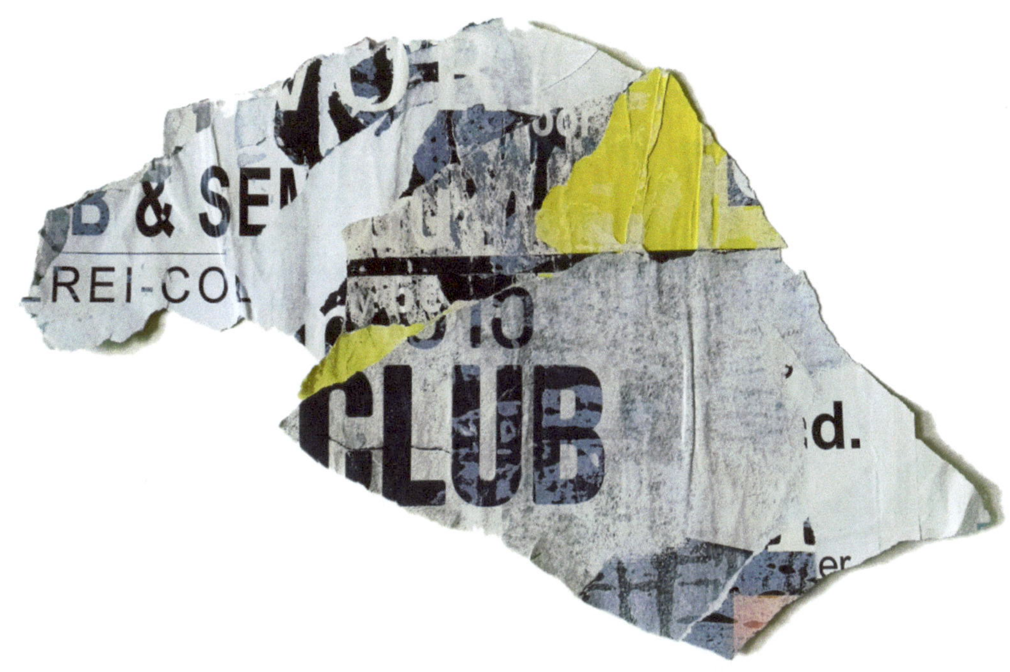

FIELD NOTES, CONT'D

She started a pot of tea."'Life isn't a racetrack. You don't zoom straight from start to finish in sequence. It's an ocean – vast, endless, full of wonders and dangers, nonlinear, mysterious, everything happening all the time."

"'What about time as our lives pass? It moves in one direction at one pace. And you **deal** in the passage of time!"

She gave a gallic shrug. "That's work, and that's not all of my life. I have noticed I am living every moment of my life all the time these days." She smiled as she got out the cups and saucers. "But I'll allow the unidirectional linear concept of time is a very convenient construct. It helps us meet for tea if we wish it."

As she sat, I handed her the other paper I had brought. "This isn't for the archive. It's for you, if you want it."

"Thank you." She looked. It was a yellowed plan view of a building, a Weimar-style beauty I had guarded from the wrecking ball – plenty of life left in it. Dr. A looked at me with a gleam in her eye. I think she understood everything in that moment, but she still played along. "What is it?'"

"It's a building I own. It's large enough for paper-based Microtemporals to do a lot of work. It was actually Lauren's idea. She wanted to be a fly on the wall at international conferences for MTs, and this is a way to make that happen. I can set up a foundation to fund the research."

"Why do you do this?" She was amazed and, I could see, happy, but just puzzled.

"I want to. Because wherever it is, beginning, middle or end, it is part of my arc. Or I should say my ocean."

There are not many knights in the world, but she and Milos and Alex strike me as three worth supporting.

More soon.

Acknowledgments

I developed my ideas about microtemporal archaeology while living and working in Berlin. I started using Berlin paper in 2013 for palimpsests and collages, work out of which this book grew. I have created a number of series that combine pieces of Berlin's paper voices to make new images, and in the course of collecting paper found fragments so beautiful I saw in them self-standing works of art, and these fragments became the backbone of this book. If enough people got fascinated by the loveliness of forgotten, discarded, and outdated paper and thought about what it was pointing to, perhaps the imaginary discipline of microtemporal archaeology would really exist. Dr. A is the voice that explains in brief a few of my thoughts about ephemera and paper and why they might be important.

Over the past few years I have lived many months in Berlin, learning the city and encountering stellar people, some of whom deserve special thanks, all of whom will almost certainly protest they had nothing to do with this project, but I ask they will take me at my word that I am in their debt and that they contributed in different ways to this work. For the good you gave me, I hope this book gives you something good back. May your kindness return to you a hundredfold.

Dr. Michael Bowdidge is a staunch advocate of my explorations and a wonderful colleague for unpacking ideas around ephemera and the hidden versus the shown. Sascha Bachmann shows me a side of Berlin I would never find on my own and fishes me out of occasional trouble with his knowledge of the city and its workings. Birgit Lachmuth is a true patron of the arts in more ways than I can count, most especially in giving me a wonderful place to land and in her wholehearted advocacy of my work, as well as her indulgence in the matter of strange papers that inevitably follow me to my room, knowing I will sweep up.

The Berlin School of English taught me to find the sense of things when they come to me in other languages. The Transart Institute supported my graduate studies in Berlin. Klaus Knoll opened the door for me and many other artists, leaving us room to find our own way to walk through it.

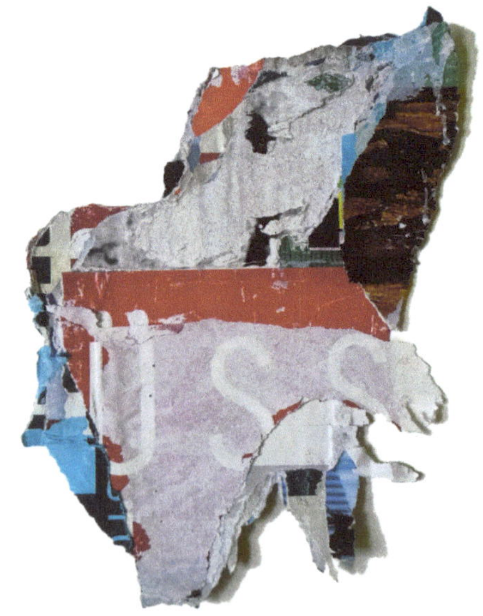

Peter Blair's generous support at a critical moment has yielded orchards of fruit. Nuno Vicente rescued an orphan project and gave the palimpsests their start at João Cocteau Kunstraum in the dead of winter 2013. Without Peter and Nuno, I doubt this book, or any of my major work of the past three years, would exist. Dr. Meredith McClain gave enormous encouragement and support in my toughest season as well as an introduction to Quedlinburg and its artists. She is unfailingly kind in her unparalleled hospitality and her ebullient advocacy of my work. Dermis Leon gave me essential critique and advice when I switched media. She is always first to encourage me to explore the possibilities of my work more rigorously, and was at my side when it was time to talk about the work in public. Eva Moll at Art von Frei and Ismael Duá at Das Kapital enthusiastically supported my experiments in paper and offered me fora in which to share my work. Heidi Russell and the International Women Artist's Salon gave me the microphone and introduced me to a worldwide audience on the air.

Michael Brune, my brother on the ground, taught me German slang and introduced me to the Tacheles, the Neue Heimat, Engelbecken, and so many other places and things adoptive Berliners ought to know. Dr. Brian Cusack gave me a new voice. Stefan Heusser gave me critical insights into street art, among other essential things. Alex Lorenz and Justin Paresky graciously served as inspirations for Dr. Lorenz and Dr. Minas. Prof. Dr. Karl Kohut welcomed me on my first visit to Berlin. He is a formidable scholar and a generous friend, hearing out my ideas and pointing me to sources that have guided my research since our initial meeting in 2010. I feel gratitude to my second heimat, the city of Berlin itself, for speaking from the walls every day and for all that beautiful paper.

More thanks than I can say to my parents, Prof. Dr. Edward George and Cecilia George for their eagle eyes and for their enduring support, love and concern in all things. Bless you.

Endless and limitless gratitude and love to Scott Billups, for your endless and limitless love and support, and for all our adventures, past, present and future. Blessings on your sweet head. <38X

--Paula Billups
October 2015

About the Artist and Author

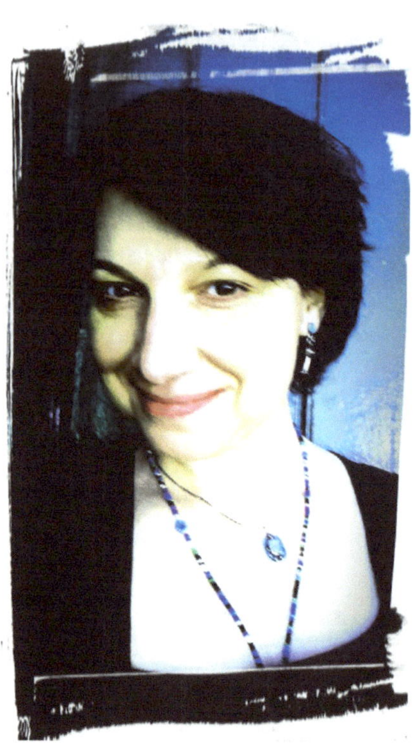

Paula Billups is a fine artist who works in various media. Since her first visit to Berlin in 2010, she has returned many times to delve further into her work and to strengthen her ties with her own community there. With PAPER, she offers a love letter to her second home and a postcard from the streets of Berlin to her readers. Using scraps of paper found on her own rogue searches for artifacts Dr. A would likely want, she creates a series of small stories around each fragment that reflects something of the character of Berlin.

Ms. Billups holds an MFA from the Transart Institute in Berlin, a BFA from the Lyme Academy College of Fine Art in Connecticut, and a BA in English from the University of Texas. When she was a child, her father took her to summer digs with the Texas Archaeological Society, and for one memorable summer she was a lab assistant at a Paleolithic dig in Texas.

She has exhibited in numerous countries and has held residencies in Germany and Italy. Her work is in various private and institutional collections.

For more about the author, visit her website at www.paulabillups.com

www.ingramcontent.com/pod-product-compliance
Lightning Source LLC
LaVergne TN
LVHW070203110826
845147LV00002B/487

* 9 7 8 0 6 9 2 5 4 0 5 6 5 *